Meeting the PETERSON'S

Daniel Patterson

To order additional copies of this book, contact:
Xlibris
844-714-8691
www.Xlibris.com
Orders@Xlibris.com

ISBN: Softcover   978-1-6698-6229-1
         EBook   978-1-6698-6228-4

Print information available on the last page

Rev. date: 01/09/2023

CONTENTS

CHAPTER ONE

Meet the Peterson's

Hello my name is Tommy Peterson. I'm 43 years old and my family and I just moved to Alabama from Texas. It is a whole lot of differences between goings from flat country to mountain country. If we didn't move to the hill country. My son Bubba was now 28 years old met the most beautiful young girl in the world. Her name was Bevely. Bubba and Bevely then dated for about a year before deciding to get married and start a little family of their own. That following year on February 5th, 1997 they welcomed a baby boy whom they named Robert David Peterson. Following Robert David's birth his grandpa Tommy Peterson would come over and read one or two stories from the Bible to him. His favorite story from the Bible though was the Good Samaritan and then he asked grandpa how he could be like him. A year later they decided to move down South to Louisiana where Bevely's grandparents lived. As they were packing everything up for the big move the phone rang and it was Beverly's Doctor reminding her of her appointment. When they went to see the doctor the next day they were surprised to find out that she was going to have twin girls. The girls were born on October 24th 1998 right after the moved. Their names are Wanda Marie and Daisy Mae. They were also happy when we told them that we were moving right around the corner and Robert would go knock on the door and see them whenever he wanted to.

4

Bevely always wanted a restaurant of her own so we built a little restaurant business and called it Bevely's (Bar and Grill). It was a family run business so Bubba called some of his uncles to help. Bubba called two of his uncles that he knew what it took to run a restaurant. Uncle Delbert knew about keeping up with the supplies and the food and then there was Uncle Harry he was the Chef of the family. As the children were growing up they were always getting into trouble around the restaurant. Bubba and Bevely would call their great grandparents Etta and Lewis Buffay to watch them for a little while they were at work. Sometimes grandma would let me help her cook while great grandpa Lewis would be reading to the girls. Sometimes after playing he would get tired and fall asleep Sitting in his sofa. When the girls would get through playing with their toys they would start coloring in their coloring books that they brought with them to their house. While Bubba and Bevely would be at the restaurant on Monday nights because they would be very busy because they would have football game nights. They asked the customers what they would like to have to eat on Monday nights. They said hamburgers and hotdogs so they had to make sure they had a good supply of them; on every Monday night because it would be football game night. The kids were growing up and were beginning to start school. Bubba would take them to school while Bevely would go get things ready at the restaurant. When she would get there she would find Uncle Harry already getting the food bar fixed. Uncle Delbert would always stay in the kitchen making sure that they had all the food that they needed. Daisy would always be outside on the tire swing that Bubba put out about a month ago while Wanda was at Grandpa George's with her puppy Rocky. He would follow her around the house like they do when they are puppies.

CHAPTER TWO

Inspired by Grandma

Apple pie Recipe
• Apples
• Butter and flour
• Sugars
• Pie Crust

FLOUR

Robert was inspired to go to culinary school by his great-grandma Etta. Robert turned 25 years old on February 5th a week later after his great-grandma passed away. She taught him a lot about cooking and making desserts. Robert also has two uncles that are working for his mother in her restaurant.

After Robert started College he met a girl and her name was LeAnn. They started dating and after three years of dating they decided to get married. After getting married they decided to move back home and help his mother with her restaurant. He could also learn some more things about cooking from his uncle as well as how to manage the business. When his mom was out of town on business trips. Robert and his wife LeAnn would always be writing down new recipes to try at the restaurant. After writing all of the different recipes down he showed them to his mom and she would tell him that he should show them to his uncle Harry because he was the Chef of the family. He showed him all of the items he would need and then he started to show Robert how to prepare the food. When the day was over they started home. They stopped by the grocery store to pick up a few things for the next day. LeAnn does all of the shopping for the items that we would need. Before Grandma passed away that year she would write down and show Robert some ingredients to add to her Apple pie recipe to make the customers come back for more. They would always have to make sure they had apples. They also tried other desserts like blueberry cobbler, blackberry cobbler, and peach cobbler to shake things up a little bit. Thursday LeAnn and Robert could only work half a day because she had a doctor's appointment. She found out she was going to have a baby boy whom they named Ralph Wayne Peterson. When Ralph was born he would always get into trouble just like his dad when he was young. He would always need help with watching him while he was at work so he would call up his sister Wanda to come over and help watch Ralph when she had a day off. Robert would always help his uncle Harry Buffay get the food ready for the next day.

When Robert didn't have to go to work he would spend time at home with his wife and son. When he would get home he would he would get Ralph's favorite toys and start playing with them on the floor with Ralph while mom would relax. Sometimes she would fall asleep on the couch and Robert would have to cover her up. While she slept we would go to the restaurant and Robert would show Ralph what his uncle Harry Buffay and his uncle Delbert Buffay would be doing. Mom would be at the house waiting for us to get back home. Every now and then Robert's mom and dad would come over and visit for a little, while Robert and his dad would talk about what they were going to be doing the next day. The children are up in age and Wanda has a job working at a bakery just around the corner.

Chapter Three

The Pris Pot Bakery

There is a bakery right around the corner from the restaurant the person who runs the bakery is Mrs.Pris. The bakery is called The Pris Pot Bakery. Bubba and Bevely are friends with Mrs Pris's family. Her father Mr. Aldridge helps her at the bakery. Mr.Aldridge is a retired Oil Tycoon and her mother Ellie Mae Aldridge is a retired school counselor. Mrs. Pris makes her famous chocolate chip cookies from time to time. A very good friend of Bubba's from the military came in one day. They started talking and they went to the bakery to have a cup of coffee and he tried one of her chocolate chip cookies. He told Bubba that was the best cookie he had ever eaten. Mrs. Pris always loved writing down new recipes especially ones to try in the bakery because she knew if she tried it in the bakery that Bubba's friend Lieutenant Stumpy would be there to try it. After he tried them he decided that he wanted to ask her out on a date so he did. They came to my wife's restaurant, Bevely's (Bar and Grill) just around the corner.

They dated for about a year and decided to get married. A year later they had a little girl and they named her Alison Wendy Stumpy. During combat in the military Bubba saved Stumpy's life. About a year later he retired from the military as well. Bubba was just glad they got out. Alison Wendy loved to help her mom bake cookies and learn the tricks of the trade of baking cookies and cakes like her mom.

A year later the Stumpy's had another baby girl and they named her Taylor Stumpy. Taylor loved the outdoors and she would always bring her mom a flower to put in a vase to pretty up the bakery and make it look nice.

People would come talk about the oil tycoon with Mr. Aldridge and he would start telling stories about his old job.

CHAPTER FOUR

Meeting the Stumpy's

Buford and Ellie Mae Stumpy are the proud parents of Buford Oliver Stumpy Jr. When he was in the military he was a Lieutenant and everyone would call him Lieutenant Stumpy now his dad had a lot of trades and his favorite was working on the neighbors old cars. His main trade though was making barrels for Uncle Judd Wilkerson. He learned how to make moonshine from his papa. He put the moonshine in the barrels that Stumpy's dad made. Buford Oliver Stumpy Jr. always watched Uncle Judd and papa make the moonshine their favorite flavor was blueberry moonshine. Stumpy would always bring some from Tennessee all the way down to Louisiana when he would come visit us.

While he was gone his wife and kids would be at the bakery making cookies. My daughter Wanda is always taking notes and writing new recipes down to try at the restaurant. Lieutenant Stumpy's dad is always at home working on a project. His wife Ellie Mae always needs an old chair fixed so Mr. Buford is always gluing them back together so they would have enough for company when they would come over or when the grandkids would come and play in the yard now papaw that's what the kids called Stumpy's dad they would always tell them not to go the mountain without them because there is no what is up there. Now everyone knew a little about the Wilkerson family household. There cousin Maybell loved to do art so when they would get to go see her they would always look and see all of her beautiful artwork that she had done she was working on a beautiful project when we got there. It was a picture of the outdoor scenery.

While we were there watching her one of their great-uncles was there playing the guitar and then he also played the Harmonica as well. Our kids would listen to the music for hours while they were watching their cousin Maybell draw. He told us that he would also play music for people walking around in the park.

CHAPTER FIVE

Daisy was inspired by Maybell

Daisy was inspired to do art from the time we spent up in the Tennessee Mountains at Judd Wilkerson's house. Watching Maybell draw scenery. Daisy was amazed at her artwork that she spent many hours up on the mountains trying to draw a picture of what she was looking at. One day Robert and LeAnn were walking by and saw his sister drawing a picture of a bridge over a stream of water. Everywhere she goes she now has a drawing pad and a pencil in her pocket. On her birthday I surprised her with a little pencil bag with pencils and eraser's in it. Every now and then Daisy would go to see Maybell about drawing other projects. Daisy and Maybell would go on a quest. They would find different things to draw they were walking along and came upon a mountain scene. I couldn't believe how good she was getting at it. One day she decided to enter one of her drawings in a contest and she won first place that got her an art scholarship at Drew University (Madison, NJ). She finished college and became a well-known art teacher.

When she would come home her mom would always need help at the restaurant. They added on to the restaurant because it was now becoming too crowded and we also added a small bar in it. Now it hasn't changed very much since I was a little girl. They still had Money night football game nights and hamburgers and hotdogs they were also rooting for their favorite football teams. My dad would be there with one of his friends up at the bar for a drink. At night when we were done Blake would be cleaning the tables and sweeping and then he would mop the floor. After everything was done we would go home and relax. The way that Daisy could relaxed was having a pencil and paper and something to draw.

After Blake would get through with his work he would call it a night. When he would leave he would go over to see Taylor.

Printed in the United States
by Baker & Taylor Publisher Services